The Book of Noob

Johan Kylander

PILOT PRESS

© Pilot Press 2011
All Rights Reserved
ISBN 978-91-976077-1-1
Printed On Demand
Graphic design by Johan Kylander
Typeset in Garamond and Fette Fraktur
Final artwork by Karolina Söderbäck Brantskog
Edited by Richard Malkoski
Pilot Press, Päronvägen 23, 146 48 Tullinge
www.pilotpress.wordpress.com

To NOOb, wherever you are

CHAPTER 1

Creation. The Dawn of N00b. First Flight. Tail Wheel.
Torque. Stall. The first Hanger fly-through and the first
Tree. Online. RTFM. In the Weeds. First Contact. Bandits.
Turning. Burning. Trim. Rebirth. Despair. The Gods speak
again. More Despair. Happily ever after.

In the Beginning there was Light in Texas, Pixel upon Pixel of Light, and then there were Aeroplanes. And when there were Aeroplanes there was great Joy upon the Earthe and above the Earthe, for then there were also Individuals of great Daring and Confidence to pilot them. They were known amongst themselves as Fighter Pukes, yet to the Appearance of Gods they were all N00bs. And it was good.

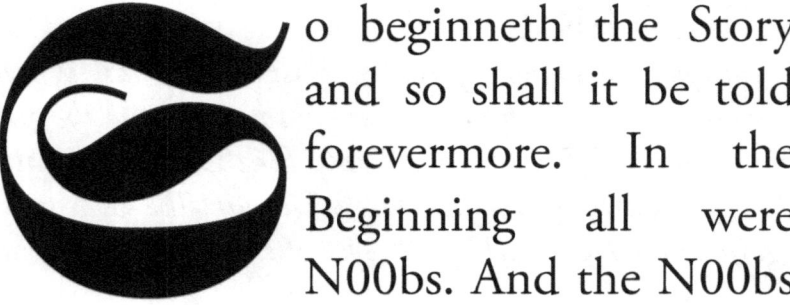o beginneth the Story and so shall it be told forevermore. In the Beginning all were N00bs. And the N00bs begot a second Generation of Pilots, bearing the Family Name and in all respects similar to their Forefathers, and that too was good.

n the first Day of Installation the Fighter Pukes bang'd their Chests and strapp'd their Bodies into Machines of wondrous Matter, to prove their Mettle forthwith. Yet despite Curses of increasing strength and foulness their Craft refused to leave the Earthe, as if these winged Beasts of Destruction had a longing too strong for the sharp Embrace of solid Matter. Ground Loope upon Ground Loope was performed to the cries of "WTF!!", and "What am I doing wrong!", and "Why won't this Damned Plane fly??!?", for they were N00bs, and N00bs knoweth not better.

rom the Heaven boom'd forth a mighty Voyce, scaring the N00bs half out of their Wits and impressing them forever with their lack of Knowledge in matters pertaining to flight. "Harken to Me, thou N00bs! Thou shalt lock thy Tail Wheel afore attempting to slip the surly Bonds of Earthe". So did the N00bs lock their Tail Wheels, and it was immediately perceived as good. Yet the surly Bonds remain'd unbroken and there was a great gnashing of Teeth upon the Earthe.

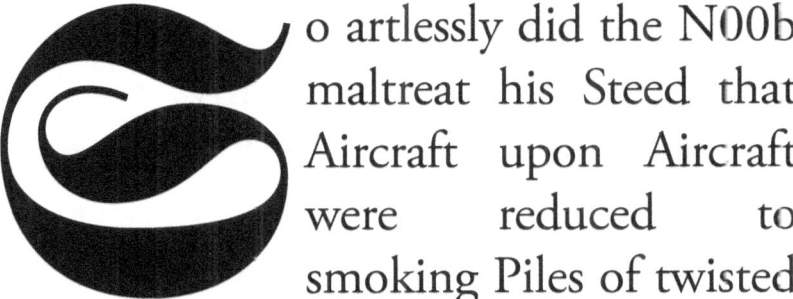o artlessly did the N00b maltreat his Steed that Aircraft upon Aircraft were reduced to smoking Piles of twisted Aluminium until the Voyce boom'd forth again, this time with Mirth but poorly concealed. "Thou shalt bear in Mind the awesome Power of thine Engine for it createth Torque of considerable strength, sufficient to throw thee Cheek first unto the Ground. Harness this Power with judicious application of Rudder and counteract thy rolling tendency with opposite Aileron". Thus did the N00bs practice much until they could safely throw themselves into the Air several meters before encountering further Complications. For they were well and truly N00bs.

 greate kaboom was heard many a time as N00b after N00b slamm'd catastrophically with great random into the unyielding Ground, hardly mask'd by shrieks of Horror and Consternation. Hence the Voyce boomed "N00b! Thou shalt not pull so mightily on thy Stick afore thine Airspeed is sufficient for Flight, lest thou be punish'd swiftly by fearsome Stall to thence flutter harshly to the cold hard Matter. Thou Fool! Stabilize thy Craft to comfortable Speed and then thou mayest Maneuvre". Thus He spake and the N00b obey'd until he was no more an Earthebound N00b but a flying N00b.

n wings of horrific destruction recently tamed the Fighter Puke lofted himself into the Skye. "Yay! I'm UP! Henceforth am I no longer a N00b! Look out! Here I come!" croonéd he and aim'd his nose through the nearest Hanger. Many a time distinctly dented and charr'd it was before the N00b rushed giddily through its wide yet narrow Span, to embrace the omnipresent Destroyer, the Tree, in spectacular Explosion, Conflagration, and precipitation of constituent Parts. And so N00b remain'd a N00b, to the great Entertainment of Gods and Spectators.

o came the wondrous Day — verily, the First Day, the Day of his real Birth — when N00b pressed the tantalizingly glowing Button that spelt "Play Online". And lo! he did behold a Land of plenty, where Fighter Pukes galore were already aloft and seeking each other's swift Annihilation. Humbled by this presence of other, hysterically vocal N00bs, this N00b did venture out to a faraway Field called Cambrai or Bertrix to try his Luck and his Guns. Up he went and all the Angels of the Skye hummed in unison. "W00t!" was his first utterance, and "WTF!" his second, as the evil Vulcher from Hell swept down and smote him a vicious blow. "Haha!" croon'd he, "N00b! Check thine Six before takeoff or I shall smite thee a second time!". Much distressed and lusting for Revenge did the N00b thus check his Six, and seeing nothing but a great big Seat took off again into the waiting Guns of Vulcher.

T his was not in the Manual which I did not read", cried the N00b and loudly bemoaned his Fate many a time in succession until his Brethren from rear Airfields did come to his succour and chase'd away the wily Vulcher.

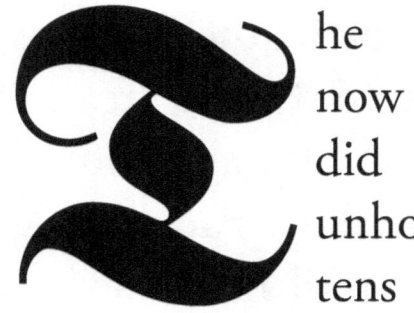he multilayered Skye now clear'd, the N00b did fly away at the unholy altitude of several tens of meters, only barely avoiding cutting the Grass on a certain popular Hill, so resplendent in gaily colored pieces of various shattered Aircraft. "So this is what it's like to be a Fighter Puke" extolled the N00b, happily testing his Guns for all to see. On his next sortie he tested not his Guns like so no more, and thus the sneaky Swooper did in fact not see him so easily thereafter. "Verily now am I a Fighter Puke, for now I know when not to phyre my Guns!" cried the N00b. "Nay", the Gods of the Skye and the High Domain retorted, "thou art naught but a Weedklipper N00b". And there was much squinting and grimacing below.

lying low over the eternally Green Pastures didst the N00b now spy an Airplane with a strange Halo glowing ever brighter. "Ye Gods, what hast thou set in my path? This Apparition is like unto nothing I have ever seen" he muttered, and emptied his Guns for King and Country in what perchance might be the right direction. Unleash'd he marvellous Thunder, watch'd he the pearly lines of sweet Tracer arcing toward the strange Shape, yet falling curiously short. "WTF!!! Why doth he not fall down in fiery Flames such as I did not so long before??!?! Crud and nerf!!! These Guns are teh Ghey!!?! I'm a Fighter Puke and these Frikken Guns are no good!", yell'd he and pounded his Temples in consummate frustration. "Nay, thou art no Fighter Puke until thou knoweth thine Enemy from thine Friend" chuckled the Gods above and sped mightily away upon their double-digit Missions.

ext upon his Trail of Misery came actual Contact form'd as zings and pings unto his Aircraft. "WTF!!?" he shouted yet again and threw his Crate into wild evasives. So pitiful were they seen from the other end of the Gun that all the Tissues in the World could not wipe away the Tears of Laughter of the opposing Pilot, though they did bring unto our N00b a brief respite. "Where the Billy Blue Blazes did he come from??!!?!" cried the N00b, "I was certain that the Skye was clear, naught could I see howsoever much I look'd!". "Whence didst thou look?" ask'd his fellow N00bs, fully anticipating the reply: "Why, forward of course, how else would I know where to fly?". Rolling on the badly swept Floor and clutching their Stomachs in painful Laughter didst the Gods of the Skye then declare "Thou N00b! Thou must cast thine eyes across the entire Skye at all time, many a time in rapid succession, never slacking, without fail, else shalt thou be smitten without Ceremony. Those whom thou seest not canst thou not combat - lose thou not sight lest thou loseth the fight!

o when the foul Enemy did come upon him a second time, the N00b pull'd mightily back upon his Stick and suffer'd another weird Experience - the World went black as Pitch yet though the throb of Engine remain'd constant. "Yea! Verily am I now a Fighter Puke for I knoweth how to evade mine Enemy!" shouted he. "Nay, yet art thou not a Fighter Puke, thou art nothing but a flaming N00b" came the swift reply from the lofty Heights, and verily, the dreaded Skulls grinn'd at our N00b again. "Thou remainest a N00b, for thou knowest not that thy Maneuvre must be like flowing Water and Woman's Temper: hard to predict and ever shifting". Thus watch'd the N00b his blazing demise with mixed Emotion, vowing Someday to fly like the Gods a-yonder.

On his next Engagement the N00b harkened to the Words of Wisdom and cautiously handled his Aircraft. A trifle too cautiously perhaps, for it took the Enemy not long to seize such a gallant Offering. Desperate with Fear and Humiliation the N00b shouted for Advice, to be told to "Turn and Burn!". Of Burning he knew far too much already, yet precious little of the previous. Circle after Circle did he turn, the Enemy in hot Pursuit and snapping at his Heels. "Ye Gods!" he yell'd, "Verily am I turning for King and Country, yet this evil Bastard will not yield! And do I not fly the most turningest Plane of all already?!?!".

Thus spake the booming Voyce, "Thou shalt always be trimmed so that even when climbing, diving or fighting thou canst release thy Grip on the Stick without immediately departing from thine selected Attitude. Thou who never trims shalt be smitten without effort by thy correctly trimmed Opponent and thus shalt thou shout "WTF!! No WAY! How did he do that??!?" a thousande times afore thou learnest the Secret of Trim".

n that moment was born the "T&B N00b". Lengthily, at least according to his Standards, and lustily did he henceforwarde cast himself with abandon into any old Furball, a Concept harkening back to ye olde Days when Naphtaline-drenched Fighting-cats were set alight and tossed into a Ring, there to rip each other asunder, Fangs out and Hair aphyre. "I'm a Fighter Puke and I'm oh-kayee, thou art mine Enemy and thou smellee!" roar'd the N00b, spraying and praying that his Shots would hit something other than thin Air and himself something other than the Ground. And it was good.

et even so was something still amiss! Never did his Phyre connect properly and never did he score anything other than Enemy Aircraft "damaged". He had yet to witness an Opponent break out in Phyre under the Hail of his Guns. So mortified was he by this failure that he approach'd one of the lesser Gods, asking him for Advice. He had none to give, except "Get thee yet closer still, thou N00b!". These Words echoed worthlessly in his Skull, for even though he pushed his Throttle Quadrant fully forward could the N00b never seem to get close enough to the elusive Enemy. "Oy vey! Woe is me! Mine aircraft is too slow, the Enemy too fast, my Guns so nerf'd and pork'd, never shall I be a Veteran or Demi-God! Woe is me! Where is the unsub Button?" he would lament in moments of utter Despair.

In this moment of utter Need and Dejection did the God's Benovelence shine upon him, bathing him in the bright Light of Insight and burning away the Fog of Uncertainty. They said: "N00b! Thou must apply Lead Pursuit! With Pure Pursuit wilt thou never close with thine Enemy! Aim thine Aircraft in front of the elusive Enemy, towards the Place in the Skye whereunto he is travelling, not directly at him, and thus shalt thou gain Closure upon him even when thy Aircraft is slower than his! Capisce?". The N00b pondered the truth of these Words at great length with Mouth agape and his Hands describing various Trajectories, eventually coming to the Conclusion that verily the Gods spake from immense Authority. And thenceforth it was very good.

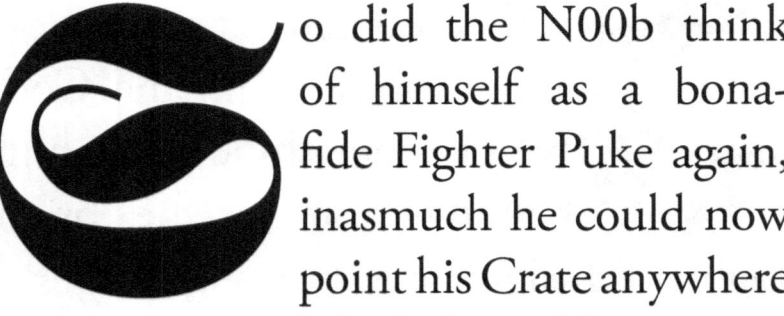o did the N00b think of himself as a bona-fide Fighter Puke again, inasmuch he could now point his Crate anywhere in the Skye and find the golden Vector of pertinent Closure, though it did take many a painful visit by the dreaded Skulls and many a Negotiation of the Graphic User Interface to become airborne again. He would scream "Whee-ha! Look out for the Fighter Puke and his awesome Lead Pursuit!", except when instead he produced a much-feared Over-shoot before the Muzzles of his Enemy. "Ha! Thou art not a Fighter Puke! Thou art but an Overshooting N00b without Class or Knowledge of the Dark Art of Lag Pursuit!" chuckled the Gods and again made strange motions with their Metacarpal Extremities for his Erudition.

ith new-found Zeal and Energy did the N00b cast himself into ever yet more cataclysmic Furballs, there to apply various amounts of Lead, Lag and Pure Pursuit. Mightily did he toil and sweat, many were the Hours slaved away in constant Agony, many were the Tears of Exhaustion and Humiliation, until finally did the Penny drop. "Woweee... I must not always point my Gunsight on mine Enemy, but I can actually", he paused to gasp, "release a Fraction of Elevator pressure to glide beyond and over my Prey, then to slash in on him with a fantastic Lead solution! What ho!". And thus for a time did he live happily, and it was good to behold.

---¤¤-Ô-¤¤---

CHAPTER 2

Revelations. Landing Gear. Pilot Error. Deliverance. Hopes Dashed. The Gods lay down the Law. The Nerf Brigade. Revenge double-dashed. Stat-Ho's. Travails. Nosebleed. Go diving down. Number of the Beast. Uber N00b. Wing'd Man.

As the N00b progressed over the first Hurdle of Learning he became accustomed to looking out for himself in other directions than through the Gunsight; he managed to takeoff without crashing nearly every time; he found that Trees and Shrubbery were made of particularly tough Material not to be messed with; he learned that Otto the AI Gunner would plink him every time even through Buildings with unfailing accuracy excepting if he was in a Stuka turning very slowly on the Deck; he began to understand that Energy is not merely something thou getést from a Candy Bar and promptly forgetest in thine Lint-filled Pocket - in short, through the event of every single Sortie a new Revelation would dawn upon him. And he took that as good and true.

With increasing alacrity and frequency he would shout "Rut-Roh! Teh Pwn! Here comes the Fighter Puke to save the Day!", yet on every occasion something inexplicable would cause him to end his Sortie in abundant Flames, as a meteoric Projectile, in jaggede multicolored Pieces thrust forcefully into the Ground, or as all of the preceeding combined. And the Gods would snicker and cackle "NAY, a Fighter Puke art thou Not! Thou art naught but a N00b with scant Experience in the Art of Five-dimensional Combat. Thou hast yet to learn to use thine Eyes and thy Braine properly so that thou mayest employ thine Takeoff Gear twice in the same Sortie". And the N00b said: "Whut?".

Thus pass'd the early Days in World War Two Online, the N00b meeting other N00bs in the Skye and sometimes gunning them down, sometimes being gunned down by them. As usual however, the very vast Bulk of Casualties were suffer'd from that most dastardlie of Enemies known as Pilot Error. This Pilot did hugely induce the N00b with over-zealousness in filling his Targets with Lead unto the Point of Collision; caus'd him to pull and to push on the Joyous Stick with such vigour that again he be visited by the Skulls; tempted him to look over his Shoulder when flying but scant metres over the ever-unyielding Ground and causing him to become the subject of that great Publick Entertainment known as the Lawn Dart; assur'd him that a Split-Esse could be performed safely from a scant 200 feet of Altitude; and many other funny Pranks.

About this time the Gods in their lofty Abode issued forth a much-awaited Announcement: the Poor-Cousins of France were to be gifted with a new-fangl'd Machine of greate destructive Power, immediately doubling their available Fighter types. The Machine was to be delivered "soon™", and so happy were the French N00bs that they fêted on braised Sheep and somersaulted with joy. Alas, they ran out of Sheep in short Order, for "soon™" was not in fact "soon™" at all but "much later" or at the very least "not right now, but quite soon" or even "actually, not right now, but eventually" and even the French cannot party that long and so were forced back into their pokey Hawk 75's. Thus did the Gods play with their Underlings and had many a Laugh at their Expense, or so it was thought. That too was not so good, but it promised to be.

At long last the Saviour-Aircraft of the French arrived: the God-blessed, wonderfully-equipped-and-brand-spanking-new Dewoitine D.520. With greate Promise to offer the Evil Cabbage-reeking Messerschmitt 109 more than a match, the N00b lustily threw himself into the Skye again in his gleaming new Ride, there to run down and out-turn the fabulously turning 109 before inserting an ample Dose of 20 mm Hispano into his Posterior. It was not to be! "Confound it, there seems to be something amiss with this Plane!" shout'd he, for it could neither climb nor turn nor glide nor hardly be look'd out of. Alas, the Dewoitine did burn very well, and it did fall quite nicely. Thus were the already Pique-Nique-unfriendly Lawns of France strewn with many a D.520, and the manifolde gnashing of Teeth and the outrag'd wailings of "nerf!" were pitiful to beholde. And thus was Promise dashed.

n these days of Malcontente and Anxiety one Crowd stood out with yellow-nosed conspicuity. They were the 109 N00bs, a brazen, unabashed and loudmouth'd Clique of gleeful Pilots with multicoloured Signature Files of imposing design, undaunted, indeed cheer'd, by the wailings and gnashings from across the Fence. "Heh! STFU N00bs! Thou knowest not how to fight in thy new Planes yet, and thou must fly with great Energie, Wingmen and Coordination to have a chance! Thou art not proper Fighter Pukes like we! Phhbbbtt!" said they and waved manie a photoshopped Screenshot about. Such great Calamity and feuding was there that the Gods saw fit to intervene, they too extolling the Virtue of Tactics and Cooperation while at the same time roaring mightily: "THOU ART **ALL** N00BS FOR

EVER MORE unless thou dost purchase mine Book and readeth most diligently how to be 1337 like me". And that didst shut them all up, for a day or two, which was pretty good.

Amidst this unsightly Commotion an unlikely Group didst emerge, that verily praised the lambasted Dewoitine for its potent Cannon. This they used with N00bish joy and N00bish abandon to smite vaste numbers of tactically superior Panzers sitting outside their Infantry Barracks etcetera, and little didst they care for combat in the Skye. Wreck'd Panzer upon wreck'd Panzer litter'd the Field to such extent that all the Axis tactical Geniuses beleaguered the Gods Abode: through unison and Skye-rending Imitation of female Animals, and with much waving of Tinfoyl Hats and rare Documents, didst they convince the Gods that such powerful Cannon cannot exist! And not one Week gone by, that Cannon was indeed rendered harmless, while the Axis tactical Geniuses went back to strafing Allied tanks asunder in great numbers for the second consecutive year. That was neither good nor not so good but downright outrageous, and yet so it went.

oon faded but not forgotten, this Slight liveth evermore in the Minds and Hearts of greenclad N00bs. With Hearts a-boil with Anger did they vent their Frustration in Circle-strafing of every little thing grey and scurrilous. This might be a fine Idea, as it used to be, were it not for the uselessness of their Rifle Bullets, the Sawdust content of their little Bombs and the acute destructive Power of the Flak30. Subdued, these N00bs turned back to use their Wheels and Tracks and Feet, at much the same Time as the N00bs in foul Grey Planes arriv'd. Funny was it not, for they had nothing with what to Phyre back such as their Enemy could, nor was there anywhere to hide. For six whole Months. That was also quite outrageous, and yet again evenso it went.

Whatever Side or lamentable Facts one chooses to see, this is not a tale of Army Woe but of F'ing N00bs and their craving of Vets to be. Some relevance hath it though, for many of the circle-strafers claim'd the Veteran's Title, crooning "I'm so 1337 and thou art but a N00b! When thou hast a Thousande Kills like me, then mayhap thou might kiss my Boot". Upon close Inspection wert those Stats not so brag-worthy after all, consisting mainly as they did of ill-gotten counts of Squishie and Cardboard Tanks destroy'd. About this the Gods said nothing; though in Publick Light were such claims not Fame but mere total N00bery. For Pilots counteth not Trucks and Locomotives but only other Planes, such as Tradition holdeth. So it is, was, and ever shall be, and that is good.

So returneth we to the N00b and his Travails. Through all this he flew most happily, shouting "WTFG!" and "w00t!" and "WTF!??" at various times, trying hard to avoid the Sucker-Traps, the Evil Foe, the Unobtanium Trees and the still Stone-hard Ground. And it was mostly good.

ne Day (perhaps in March) the N00b felt something snap, his Office now lit with saintly clarity. "Wait a minute..." he said, and ponder'd 'pon a fleeting Thought: "Those guys that fly above me, why, I almost never see them burn!?!". He scratched his sparslie stubbl'd Chin and (drumroll, crank up the saintly lights) breathed his Mind: "Mayhap I too should fly that high?". So on his next Sortie he gave it a Shot and climbed to 2000 Meters, though Nosebleed didst he get and pure Oxygen made his Eyes go still. "Wow... I can see for Miles and Miles, and even choose what Foe to fight! 'Tis indeed a mighty thing to have, this Altitude!". Of course he was promptly shot by other Pilots doubly wise, for they came in at 3,000 Meters or more. And while that hurt, it was essentially good.

Thus for every time Replaned, he added 'nother thousand Meters on the Clock, for through this Year's Travails he learnt that nothing hurts so much as an Ego bruised. Yet Altitude by itself was to small avail when at the Front he didst arrive - for now he flew ungodly high and all his Fodder were down below! And many a time did he say unto himself, "A-diving down I go!", only to smack into the Ground anon. Strange it was and all didst he blame 'pon his Steed, 'til the Gods spoke down unto him, "N00b! Harken thee well unto this! Whenst thou goest diving down from greate Altitude, thou must chop thy Throttle and trim to front lest thou imitate the great Lawn Dart: Speed is good though only in fair measure, and thou must never throw thyself past VnE". This the N00b did grasp, and it was good.

Slowly didst the N00b progress, on every Hop learning something new. For instance, many a time did he hear the strange Outcry "6!" or "666!" or even "N00b 6!", thinking nothing of it first and then of big-Chested Women, shortly 'fore the Skulls arriv'd. Piece by Piece he glean'd that this dost mean he was in mortal Danger, and 'pon hearing the Devil's Number, he cast his Crate over and under as soon he could. Then he learn'd that his joyous Stick could verily be moved in all Directions. "My Lord!" exulted he, "'tis wondrous how fun this be! Chasing Enemy by pulling hard is NOT the only way to go! Yet may I still become a revered Puke!". At this of course the Gods snigger'd smugly, "Ya, Grasshopper, a proper Fighter Puke mayest thee eventually be, but first thou must retract thy takeoff Gear". This the N00b found slightly disturbing, for what Earthely purpose may that fill?

Year gone by and N00b was he still. Not content with shooting Squishies, he looked far and wide to find other Treats. Through much piloting hither and yon, and much looking to the left and to the right, to the heavens and the Earth below, learn'd he to find a tasty Snack in almost every flight. These were brown and strangely shapen, flying slowly and somewhat straight - ideal for N00b to try his luck. Many a munchy Blenheim didst he fry, and easy was it too. Further yet he ventured out, learning that the less they moved, the easier they'd be to kill. Thus he found a score or more, though following an easy pass through Shot and Shell, N00b was sure to catch an angry Mob much intent on having his Hide. By trial and Error he found a Cure: running

bravely without a Worry. Thus he sang "La-la-la-la-la, verily now am I a Fighter Puke!" though the distant Voyce of Gods yet whispered, "Nay, yet art thou naught but an uber N00b. In manly Combat must thou prevail, and often too, afore thou mayest call thyself a Fighter Puke". And this did gnaw mightily upon our N00b.

"If Uber N00b I be, why can I then not shoot that elusive Spitphyre, or kill the evil Charcane?" lamented N00b in Publick Places. Much Laughter did his Words provide, yet Answer was promptly given: "Fool! Thy 110 is but a Piece of Junk, it cannot hold a Candle to the Wunderplanes of thine Enemy! First must thou find a Wing'd Man, and fly much in concorde with him". So he did, though Wing'd Men were few and far between, and much waiting and seeking wert not his Ticket. On such occasion as he did have this Wing'd Man however, he did live somewhat longer and evenso if not by much, 'twere at least somewhat the more glorious. And that was good and held some Promise.

or many months thereafter didst the N00b make a conscious Effort of finding a Wing'd Man on his flying Endeavours, though the Essence of Wingmanship eluded him still. First of all he did have the almost Insuperable Difficulty of keeping visual Contact with his ostensible Wing'd Man, leading to many a laboured situations trying to reconnect. "Uh… Where art Thou?" he might say, and upon getting an Update of Position he would be none the wiser for it. "This dastardly microscopic Map showeth not the names of which Thou speakest! FFS! Stupid game!" would he wail, and bemoan his Navigational Inadequacy. Thereupon the Voyce of Gods again rent the multilayered Skye: "N00b!

Thou must download and print a Map of the whole World, and thence imprint various Landmarks in Thy Thick Skull so that Thou art nevermore at a loss for Position. Sheesh!" Finding the Golden Trove of Five he didst so, and it was extremely good.

et the Challenge of sticking to his Wing'd Man was not immediately relieved by this Cartographic addition. For looking out of his Office in various Directions, keeping his Aircraft on an even Keel AND following his Wing'd Man through turns and multifarious Gyrations did impose the severest of Strains upon his Attention. Thus he found himself looking mostly forwards again, vowing to keep his Eyes glued on that other Plane come what may. Of greatest vexation was the embarrassment of overshooting his Leader and promptly losing Sight in the frantic attempt to regain Position, then the debilitating Realisation of finding himself all alone in an empty Skye. So much did he Curse his Fate that the very Air of his Office turned Blue, shortly before being visited by Ye Olde Skulls and Crossbones again.

his did vex our N00b unto the very depths of Despair, for had not the Gods themselves said that flying with a Wing'd Man would make him a Bona Fide Fighter Puke? Yet here was he, seeing naught but Skulls with much too alarming Frequency, even on such sorties wherein he managed to follow his Leader with some success! And so he brooded and pondered, gnashed his Teeth and even bethought himself of an Army Career yet again. "Bollocks to Fighterpuking! My God, why hast Thou forsaken me? I am in such dire Need of Knowledge, and no amount of Industry avails me!" lamented he. A great Cackle rolléd through the Tracer-burnt Skye as the Gods retorted: "Thou pitiful N00b! Merely following another Aircraft is not proper Wingmanship!

Thou must maintain Holy Separation, and employ the Voyce through it all, lest thou be aught but an Inconvenience to thy Leader. Now get thee hence and bother us no more, until thou hast learnt thy Lesson!" And the N00b took this, reluctantly and with much Trepidation, to Heart, although he had not the slightest Idea whereof the Gods spake.

hrough humble Inquiry and some Web'd Search Engines did the N00b finally get a Clue of that to which the Gods alluded. The Voyce duely installed he next endeavour'd to put it to pracktical use. Of Holy Separation he had not a Glimmering, though he was marginally confident that it would reveal itself unto him in the fullness of Time. So spake the N00b lustily through the Ether with his fellow Wing'd Men, inducing them to many a pained Sigh and irritated Silence, for the N00b could not restrain his Enthusiasm for Voyce Communication. Verily, a great span of Time did it take for the N00b to understand the proper Use and Discipline of this Tool, but by and by as he did so it became very, very good.

As this Chapter closeth, we have seen our N00b elevated from the Misery of Lone-Wolfing on the Deck to the first fumbling Steps to becoming a true Team Player. Though the Path be winding and narrow, painful and fraught with many a Trap, yon N00b hath shown himself to be in possession of that most coveted Trait the Acolyte Fighter Puke must possess in full measure: Perseverance. Bear with Us, thy most humble Narrator, as we trace further the Steps and Adventures of our N00b through his forthcoming Evolution of Skill and Awareness, even unto the Glorious Realm of version One Point Six and beyond! It promises to be pretty good.

—¤¤-Ô-¤¤—

CHAPTER 3

Overview. Unlearning. Quandary. The Gods rave. Oh-Nine. Ham and Cheese. Exultation. The Disciplinarian. Tuesday. Spitdweebs. Unlucky. Carburettor. Inverted Flight. Lament. Lambasting. The Dark Art. Split Sides. Half-Nelson. Comets.

Did he not have it all? And he did bask in Glory, and ofttimes and recurrently and with glee unabash'd did he belaud and boast of his Mighty Prowess in that Abomination of Publick Entertainment, Pleiskul, over the measly kills he garnered, to the utter Scorn and Loathing of his Peers. Wondrous Voyce Communication he had, a mighty fine Joyous Stick, Rudder Pedals even and an unlimited amount of Aircraft to wreck solely for his own Pleasure. And while all this was jolly good, he had neither Style nor Character, not the slightest glimmering of Humility or Humour. Thus bereft he could not enjoy his Game to Capacity, but spent much Time

Grunting and Cursing in impotent Anger. Yet there was Hope, for he was on the true Path of Learning, in Pursuit of the Golden Rule of Separation. And that was exceedingly good.

With Battle raging ever Bitter in the Bullet-rent Skyes of France, Belgium and other Whereabouts, the N00b, now wrap'd in potent Warplane, forgot much of his earlier Lessons, such as Humans are wont to do. Among the first of these to yield was the Urge to eschew Holy Altitude, second to that the Joy of hounding lone Infantrymen across't the oh-so-flat Terrain, third of these the Unflexibility of Unobtanium Trees, thus ending his Escapades in predictable Misery.

But what of Holy Separation, thou askest? Of what Earthly use is that, particularly since Distance is a Commodity of which one has either too much or too little, surely it is nothing to bother oneself with? So didst the N00b ask the Gods, and wearily didst they Sigh and shake their Gold-lock'd Heads at this Brazen Incompetence.

oob! Foolish Unknowing N00b! Unlearned art Thou! Hast Thou nothing seen, nothing gleaned through this Year of Furballing? Knowest Thou not the Abysmal Dread of being played for the Sucker? Hast Thou never closeth upon an Enemy without being able to bring Thine Guns to bear effectively upon him? Hast ne'er thou felt like unto Ham or Cheese inbetwixt two Slabs of Bread? That, oh Pitiful N00b, is the wondrous Realm of Separation conspiring to smite Thee!" So boomèd the Gods to the cowering N00b, and he begun to see that it might be good.

This was the Golden Age of the Run-Oh-Nine, the Uberific One-Oh-Nine, the Era of the Unbeknownst Tri-Oh-Nine, the Age of sordid Canopies-Opene'd-unto-O-so-Gamey-Vision, the Dark Age of WWIIOL when hordes of Yellow-nose'd Bastards dived down and blasted sadly Handicapp'd Opponents from their pockmark'd Runways, the futile Hammering of Cross-Eyed Ottos notwithstanding. This too was the Age when many an Opponent slipped quietly away or circumspectly donned greyish Garb instead. Verily did the Bastards laugh merrily at this and much Posturing and Crowing was noted in Pleiskul and Elsewhere on account of their wholesale smiting of hapless Victims.

So did the N00b eventually learn the Golden Rule of Separation, though in manner none too pleasant. For verily did he sucker himself to be the Ham or Cheese, or even Cold Turkey for those so incline'd, by vainly following zooming Bastards while Buddies above came booming with Nose-Guns a-twinkle. By the same Token did he finally grasp, through many a false Start, that slavishly and over-zealously following his Wing'd Man in his Attack yielded little Opportunity of his own.

uite by Chance and certainly not by Design didst he one Day delay, perhaps of Fatigue or maybe merely General Sloppiness, his pursuit of Wing'd Man. And Lo! and Behold! As Wing'd Man made his Bid and missed, the Quarry, stunned but not cowed, recover'd and gave Chase! By then our N00b was just in firing Range, and quite steadily and comfortably so. The evil Enemy thus bracket'd, he smote him with little Effort. Loudly did the N00b exult: "Wheee-Ha! Man, did you see that! Now well and truly am I a proper Fighter Puke!" Cutting across his Leader's Curve, such as he previously had learn'd, and formatting on his anxious Six, he awaited the Gods Retort: "Nay, neither a Fighter Puke nor Shit-Hot art Thou not, Thou art naught but a Lucky Puke – but decent Promise dost Thou show."

et Separation is an elusive Craft not easily master'd! On this Occasion N00b was doubly graced, for his Wing'd Man was known and feared as a Stern Disciplinarian. "N00b! Where art Thou? I cannot see thee!" said he, and yet N00b was not e'en so much as a Stone's throw away! Surely must he know that N00b clung to his Tail like puling Infant to Mother's teat! "I am here Master, following thee as thou hast instructed and as the Gods themselves have ordain'd!" the N00b hasten'd to utter. "F00l! Double-Damned and Thrice-infested N00b! When thou flyest right behind me I cannot see thee, fly thou on my Wing instead, and promptly so! FFS!" Thus did the N00b finally understand what Wing'd Men and Separation had in common.

One Day in WWIIOL, possibly a Tuesday, a most Almighty gnashing of Teeth arose from the grey-clad Camp, and a most awesomely thundering "Yahoo!" and "w0000t!" from the opposing League. For on this Day the Gods unleash'd a most conspicious and heretofore nearly extinct Species, on the unsuspecting Masses. Spitphyre did he fly and Spitdweeb wast his name. Previously confined to a Barren and far Remote Island, a good 20 minutes distant from the nearest whiff of Cordite, the Spitphyre could now be had on Continental Fields. While certain hardy Souls had heretofore braved Boredom Interminable and flown this Outrageous Distance for their 20 seconds of Eight-Gun Glory, henceforth Everyman of Centurion Rank and higher could at leisure loft on Elliptical Wings. Thus was the Spitdweeb born, and it was good.

ow facing a Foe most relentless and capable of running at near Equal Speeds, verily quite able to turn inside and perform most wicked Stunts on the hapless Run-oh-Nines, the Yellow-Nosed ones grate their Teeth and fled to the Dirty South. There did they find much easier Prey, ofttimes pathetically slow Curtiss Jobs, and so did their crowing persist unabated.. "Farking Spitdweebs! Cheating Sons of Britches art thou one and all! No one and nothing can our Equal be, so therefore leave we thou to thine own Devices and jump all over these Frigging Frogs, Tee-Hee!" quoth they. And high in their Abode did the Gods snicker and snort.

Thus the N00b continued, now well into his second Year of interminable fighting yet still incomprehensibly lacking in Rank, to find himself doing Battle in hopeless Crates against the best the Enemy could muster. Bad Luck seem'd indeed to be his Lot! While still a young Buck he struggled with the unwieldy and prone-to-flippety-flop One-Ten, for that was all he could get: though ev'rywhere he lookéd Spitphyres and Hurricanes loitered in numbers galore, in readiness to pounce, and pounce they did. Miffed, he tried his Hand on that self-same Hurricane, and found that it could neither climb nor turn nor run, even against the just abandon'd and much-malign'd 110! For it had Toothpick Wings, and that was not so good.

anifold were his Errors and small indeed his Capability, though to his credit did he have pretty good fun all the aforesaid notwithstanding. Of Laughter did he get his fair Share, both of his own and his fellow Pilots making. Recall'd he with some Mirth the time when he pushed forward his Stick of Joy to follow a diving Enemy only to find his Engine inexplicably stopping in mid-air. "WTF!" shouted he, for had he not ample Gasoline still? "Gods, vot I do? Vot I do? The Engine go poof-poof-poof! FFS!" lamented he, expecting the Gods to sneer at him or to issue forth some snide Remark. Couldst there be some tricky Selector to flip or mayhap had he accidentally fingered a Button while salivating at his quarry? "Nay, thine engine has a flotation Carburettor and cannot function in

negative Gravity, N00b!" sniggered the Gods and declaimed manie times, "Thus must thou roll inverted to pull after thy diving Foe, never push thy Stick like so". Such Wisdom the N00b crav'd, and receiv'd, at practically no cost.

erily didst manie a clue-less and class-less Wannabe attempt to flee by any means available, like unto the oft-witnessed Inverted Fool's Escape. By flying upside-down or Inverted, as the Lingo goes, such Fools found their Planes gaining up to thirty extra Kilometers per Hour of top Speed, and this was much exploited, in manner like unto the elsewhere seen Stick-Stir and the much-despised Flight of the Porpoise. Loudly bemoaned and roundly cursed wert this Practice in Publick Places yet manie were those who saw no Fault therein, though of course they said nothing thereof. Such Outrage could the Gods not abide, and great was the Joy in the Skye when Engines could finally be seen to seize and issue forth volumes of black Smoke upon such dastardly mishandling. And so Life was good again, for a while.

hile N00b kept his Conscience spick and span he nonetheless continued to suck like an open Chest-Wound, and lengthily did he bemoan and decry this sordid Fact. "Why oh Why must I suck so badly? When will I a proper Fighter-Puke be? Boo-Hoo!" Had he not learned manie a Lesson? Must he learn for ever more? "Shush, N00b!" thundered the anger'd Gods, "Thou shalt NEVER be a proper Fighter-Puke if thou cannot take a punch and carry on. Character and Fortitude must thou have - thou canst not expect to be Gifted like us. Now go use thy Brain and employest thou some Tactics". Then quoth the N00b in reply, "But, but, but, the Enemy flies so fast, and they are so manie in the Skye, and their Cannon hurt so much, that one must rejoyce if one manages to get airborne at all!" said the N00b. And properly vulched and strafed was he.

hou sorry excuse of a stinking Goat-Turd!" roar'd the Gods, "disturbest us not with such trifling Matters but learnest thee this simple Lesson: make use of other Fields farther back whereat the Enemy is not quite as plentiful. Thou must also wind thy Altimeter such as thou hast previously learn'd, and not be in such a frickin' hurry to die!" Thus spake the Gods, and the N00b saw anon that it was good. Although his time to Combat was disturbingly prolonged by several Minutes, he did get to fight for some additional Seconds before being unceremoniously slaughtered as of yore, though he complained not, for he would anyway spend manie a waking Hour in the Seat, and thus it did not overly bother him.

'was about this time that the N00b found out that running away from his Enemy usually was of no Avail, for he runneth in straight Lines while hoping fervently for his Pursuer to lose Sight or involuntarily crash into some Tree whilst giving chase. Such Hope was always in vain; indeed, the Gods hath proclaim'd, "Hope hath no place whatsoever in the Skye. Strikest thou that Thought from thy Mind, and be'st thou not afraid to fight!" And so it was, through Intervention both Gracious and Divine, that N00b learned the utility of Guts, and the dark Art of Scissors, although at first he remonstrated bitterly that such a complicated Concept must be quite difficult to learn.

ndustriously throweth he his Crate this-away and that-away in the Skye, frantically at first and desperately unto the End, while the Gods rolléd over and again in raucous Laughter. "N00b! Thine Antics paineth us much, verily, our Sides are splitting and we think we are like to burst our Spleens! Proper Scissors eludest thee still, for such haphazard Zigging and Zagging is of small Value. Thou must keep thine Enemy in view while reversing and only Zig or Zag when it is most auspicious to do so, that he may fall out of sync with thy moves. Then thou mayest wrestle him unto Death." Long did he ponder this Truth until the Penny dropp'd. And then it was wholly good.

In this and other manners did he learn the Flat and the Rolling Scissors, the Half-Nelson and the Roundhouse, the Cork-Screw and the Hammerhead, the Rabbit-Punch and the Jersey Fake-Away. While certain of these Maneuvres wert less than useful for Knightly Combat in the Skye, he argued cannily that it was better to know too much than too little. Though anyone watching might have thought that a mite of Timing and a bit of Aggression would have sufficed to rid him of pesky Enemies, rather than more bookish learning. And so he fought, well at times, and crappily at most others.

et however manie learning Opportunities he threw himself into, he would still break every one of the Seven Deadly Sins of Air Combat, on account of Foul Play by his enemies which he declaimed, or through sheer Idiocy as said the Gods. Whatever the Cause, the Result remain'd invariably the same: N00b, in a flaming Hulk, hurling himself Comet-like against the inflexible Earthe. "WTF!" exhaléd he on such occasion, and "FFS!" slipp'd his Tongue not once or twice but ofttimes in sooth, and other foul Curses too.

—¤¤-Ô-¤¤—

CHAPTER 4

Mortal Sins. Lost Sight. Disadvantage. Phyre in the Skye. Predictable. Alone. Esteem. Greed. Gratitude. Excuses. Catalog of Errors. Illumination. Oaths. B&Z N00b. Side-switching again. 1337, Pomposity. Lamentations. Tri-09. Teh Nerf.

Seven Deadly Sins of Air Combat?" asketh N00b, "I know of no such Sins?", and the Gods foameth at the Mouth in evidence of such brazen Ignorance.

Thou shalt NEVER lose Sight of thine Enemy, lest thou loseth the Fight" roareth the Gods, "Nay, seldom dost thou ever see thine Enemy approach in the first place for verily, thou lookest too seldom around thee."

hou shalt NEVER begin a Fight at a Disadvantage if thou canst help it" thundereth the Gods, "yet routinely do we tally thee as the Pouncee rather than the Pouncer".

hou shalt ONLY phyre thy Guns to Kill" shouteth the Gods, "not, like a N00b, without a Prayer at too far a Distance".

hou shalt NEVER become predict-able" cried the Gods, "for nothing gets shot down faster than a Fellow who honors his Enemy's anticipation, as thou should bloody well know!"

hou shalt NEVER fly alone" shrieked the Gods, "for while a lone fighter believes himself invincible he is verily but a Victim-to-be."

"Thou shalt NEVER overestimate thy Prowess" grimaced the Gods, "for verily it is abominably low, nor shalt thou underestimate thy phearsome Enemies until none remain and the battle be done".

"Thou shalt NEVER succumb to Greed" cackled the Gods, "for knowest thou that such slobbering Sin shall immediately be punishéd by Collision, by the arrival of Wild-Cards, and by sudden appearance of Overwhelming Opposition".

eigning gratitude though secretly overawed by such Illumination most Holy, N00b Golf-Clapped at this veritable Stream of Learning and retreated to the nearest Enemy Forward Base, there to fly lazy Cuban-Eights and shoot the Breeze with fellow N00bs, while the Flak threw foul Balls of Phyre at him and every wingéd Enemy in the Neighbourhood lick'd his Chops and pounced with Guns ablaze. Thus N00b remain'd N00b, and that was good, for such is the Order of Things in this Warped World of ours.

oor N00b! Painful is indeed his Travail and long his Suffering and Misery! Shall he forevermore be Damned and Sentenced to Dweebish behaviour? When shall he transcend and proudly call himself a Proper Fighter-Puke, fully able to take on any Foe in any situation? When shall he leave his sorry Excuses behind, his "hey no skill, I was AFK", his "WTF bloody lag!" and "Jeebus! This ramming tactic is ghey!".

is Catalogue of Errors was truly extensive, though he did snigger sheepishly when he reflected upon his early methods, yet even while he had spent oh-so-much Time in the Office of great Destruction yet still could he not avoid certain painful mistakes, such as "Colliding Mightily with Thine Enemy", or "Stalling While Too High on Final Approach with a Bagful of Kills", or "Touching the Telephone Wires at 500 Indicated". And this did he often invoke Lucifer and Ahriman, Astaroth and Asmodeus, Beherit and Baalzebub, Marduk and Mephistopheles, but all to no avail.

or every Occasion that he fell in brightly flaming jagged Pieces to the Earthe, he suffered yet more each time, finally seeing himself in Miltonian Illumination as he

"Lay vanquisht, rowling in the fiery Gulfe
Confounded though immortal: But his doom
Reserv'd him to more wrath; for now the thought
Both of lost happiness and lasting pain
Torments him; round he throws his baleful eyes
That witness'd huge affliction and dismay
Mixt with obdurate pride and stedfast hate..."

Thus didst he inexorably swell with Purpose and Longing strong enough to surmount his inbred Impatience and fearful lack of Discipline, and from then on it began to get Pretty Damn' Good.

And so betimes did the N00b swear a Greate Oathe: to depart the Fiefdom of N00bhood, to henceforth survive at any Cost, and to cast away all his weak-sauce former ways. Thus finally began he to make use of rearward Fields and to abide loftier than ever he had done heretofore. And it was good.

In his high Heaven didst he enjoye himself immensely, for up there scarcely any rose to challenge him, nay, he commandeth the Skye at every turn and could fall down mightily and sniggeringly at poor hapless Clowns far far below such as he had previously learn'd and unlearn'd. Thus didst N00b transform himself into a Bona Fide Boom-and-Zoom N00b. And the Gods looked down from their Perch and golf-clapped in approval.

Though high he flew he couldst not compete properly with the evil 109, for it turneth so devilishly well, and climbeth it like a Demon from Hell, and its Cannons were powerful still. What, asketh N00b, canst thou do if thou canst not beat thine Enemy? Thou joinest him! Thus was it so, in face of Challenge most severe, that hordes of disgruntled Pilots like N00b quietly slipp'd o'er to join the Dark Side where the Challenge to o'ercome was not quite as big. Yeaso, such is the way of the N00b.

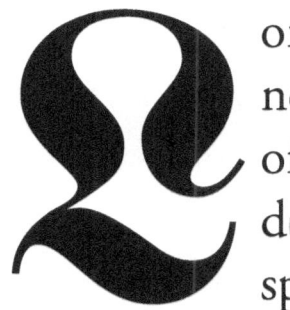ong didst he enjoy his newfound superiority. And oftimes too did he go diving down to vulch newly-spawned Enemy Aircraft like so many Baby Seals in front of their Hangers, all the while laughing heartily at the impotent Ack-Ack. Long did he strafe Enemy Tanks asunder and chase Enemy Riflemen about the near-flat landscape. And he croonéd "13337! 133337! me so 1337!" for now he did return with manie a Kill on his Tally-Sheet.

uch was his Success that he felt his Head grow large and his Heart thunder with Pride, and so did he proclaim "I am now a Fighter Puke for I have left my N00bish ways behinde!" Such pomposity, such presumptuousness, the Gods could not abide, but threw him a Bolt of blistering Rebuttal: "NAY, N00b art thou still and N00b shalt thou remain until thou knowest how to fight an even Combat to successful Conclusion without Panicking and hugging AI guns. Fighter Puke art thou not but merely a Gun and Run N00b! Penance now shalt thou make!"

ut a full a year have I play'd this Game and manie a Foe have I destroy'd", lamented N00b, "and lookest thee here at my very own gaudy Signature File of imposing Design, adorn'd with manie a Medal and Ribbon, why then can I not a Fighter Puke be? A Lieutenant General am I, though not a Vet by Gods Reckoning?" So complaine'd he and mightily wondering did he go back to his similarly be-jeweled Compadres to gang-bang and circle-strafe and otherwise indulge in Baby Seal Clubbing.

ar beyonde this rowdy Spectacle, aye, ensconced in hallowed Halls made of pure Code did the Gods loiter, and one day, quite perchance, did the Greate God Mo inspect more closely the Run-oh-nine Flight Model, and discoverd that Lo! the abomination had not two wings, but rather THREE. Thus did the Gods labor posthaste to remove this redundant wing, and forthwith presented anew the One-Oh-Nine as an Auditted Plane. And thereupon were there manifold cries of "Oy Vey!", and "Nerf!", and "Rabble-Rabble-Rabble!", and there was much wailing and gnashing of Teeth.

rom that Day forwarde did the Run-oh-Nines no longer turn so easily, and they did flutter and fall in ever-increasing numbers until the very Earthe was cover'd in itsy-bitsy, teensie-weenie M'schmitt Pieces, and the Yellow Bastards shriekéd mightily and lamented "Teh Nerf! Zis cannot be! Our Oh-Nine is now not ze turningest Plane in ze Game! How most unfair! Bias! I quit!" Manie Ye Olde Document industriously unearth'd they did wave frantically about, showing fancy Curves and Engine Test-Stand Notes, and manie were they who immediately did press the UnSub Button anon but not before whining incessantly such that none could fail to notice.

---¤¤-Ô-¤¤---

CHAPTER 5

New kites. Nurfed Spit. Franz. The Lord Saviour Curtiss.
Status Quo Ante Bellum. Ten Visions. Wuergers. Republic.
Yaks and Migs. Brolly. Horrido once more. Trains. Weather.
Formations. Purchase. Farewell to N00bs.

In that the third Year of wing'd Combat proclaim'd the High Priest of Rats that new-fangl'd Fighters of wondrous speed and weaponry would soon arrive, and Yea, a great Hullabaloo was heard in the Corps of Aviators. These new Fighters wert called Second Tier and much discussed were they in that un-mentionable Publick Cesspit called Pleiskul. These were variously the Supermarine Spitphyre Mark V, and the Spitdweebs rejoyc'd, for this Mark allegedly bore marvellous Hispanos; the Messerschmitt 109-F4, and the Luft-wobblies rejoyc'd and sniggered thunderously, for the Franz pack'd the fast-firing centerline MG-151 Motorkanone; and the Curtiss P-40 Warhawk, and thus included did the Frogs rejoyce too.

o and beholde! "Now art we truly Fighter Pukes!" croon'd the Spitdweebs and cavorted in the Skye. "Nay, Spitdweebs art thou still" cackled the Gods, "only now art thou Cannon-packing, speed-freaking Spitdweebs". Soon the formerly so boisterous S'dweebs were miffed however, for their shiny new Kite shot but Marshmallow Slugs and at the first tug 'o the Joyous Stick did they black out and fall in droves, screaming foully. "Thou art truly N00bs, for thou handlest thy new Crates without Respect" sneer'd the Gods and closed their Ears to shut out the Cacaphony of Complaint.

Likewise didst the Oh-Nine Dweebs mutter and complain, for the Franz behav'd not unto their expectations, for it too could not turn very well, even though it pack'd Wings a'thrice at least for a while. Fast it runneth however and so wert they again and forevermore known as Run-Oh-Nines, and that was both befitting and good. And so echoed their manifolde cries of "Horrido!" and lo! great numbers of dangerous Blenheims wert split asunder, and so they said "Haha! We are ze Experten Veteran Pukes and our Signature Files are so much gaudier than ze others, we are teh pwn, und thou art teh suk!"

hough in the midst of perma-looping, Cuban-Eighting, Uber-waffles with their cannon-packing Arsenal didst a most Phearful Plane plummet, Leading Edges a'flash and Hood a'twinkle. "Our Lord Saviour Curtiss!" intoned the Froggy Pilots, "Praise Our Dearest Fifty Caliber, now Gerry ain't as naughty by half!" they sang, "Our Most Holy 'Murrican Iron, we, thy most faithful Servants hail thee, O Hallowed Pee-Forty!" they croon'd and blasted 'Waffles into itsy-bitsy teensie-weenie pieces, never hesitating to Turn and Burn nor Boom and Zoom with anything in their Enemy's Inventory. And the 'Waffles shriek'd girlishly and whine'd piteously for all to hear. "Teh? Marseille shot these frikken crates down like nothing at all, why then can I not too?" and "BS!" spake they, meaning not Best Spoken nor Bravo Sheila but Bull Shite, while the Gods roll'd on the Floor suffering Cramps again.

So fought N00bs on either side as of yore, in the pixellated Skye shatter'd and rent asunder by cries of Agony and Despair. Again did N00bs in great numbers hapless fall through the multi-layered Cloud and Haze, always Comet-like, muttering the eternal "can a guy get a six-call around here or what?" and "No Way! Where did he come from?" and "this POS can't turn for shite!", such as is their Custom. And in their high Heaven didst the Gods snicker and snort, for well they knew that at level 6.2 on the Whine-O-Meter N00bs and Pukes alike are well and truly content.

hat then, thou askest, will the world be like in years to come? What Divine Steeds will grace the Skye, what tremendous Beauty will thine Eyes behold, what Promise will keep thine Interest burning clear? Advice and Comfort seekest thou, and thus the Oracle spake in Ten Visions of the Future:

ne. Glitzy new Wuergers of Doom with Kanonen a-plenty shall fall upon thee and make thy Life miserable. These will be piloted by the Wuerger Dweeb, the BFG A-Eight Dweeb and the Dora Dweeb. And slothful Spitphyres of increasingly longer Roman-Numeral-Marks will arrive to chase these Doomsday Machines from the Skye.

wo. The New Republic will rise in the West and spew forth Spamcans and Thunderbolts, Mitchells and Viermot Boeings, Fork Tailed Devils and Black Widows, and it will be very, very good... unless thou art a Kiddiekrieger or Whinewaffle.

hree. In the East the Great Dictatorship will vomit great volumes of Yaks and Migs and LaGGs and Stormoviks, and the Bad Sons of Germania will tremble in Phear for they will have little to counter the aerial Onslaught and the Hordes of Steel flooding the Plains of Prussia.

our. In a not so distant Day, defeated Pukes will bail out below a Brolly of Silk and wend their Way Home on Foot, dodging Tanks and Barb'd-wire and Landmines, armed with but a Pistol and dogged Determination to save their precious Stats.

ive. Before the End of Days Evil Experten will slice through the Skye in mighty Aeroplanes devoid of Propellors sprouting 30 millimeter Kanonen shouting Horrido! yet again. The number of the Beast shalt be "262" and it too shalt be phearsome lest it be vulchéd to Hades while low and painfully slow or when caught turning on the deck. So sayeth the Oracle and it shalt be the Truth.

ix. Terra Firma shalt become ever more detailed and induce Piloten to fly Nap Of Earthe to beholde it in all its Glory. Trains shall chugalug across the pixel'd Landscape, Tunnels shalt be bored through Mountains and the Alps shalt rise Snow-capp'd o'er the Battlefield. Sheep shall inhabit the Earthe and move about in greate Flocks, and downed Pilots will now also paddle the Ocean for hours and hours to save their precious Stats from perishing. So shall it be done, and it will be good.

Seven. Thunderstorms and Snowy Clouds, Sheets of Rain and Hail, Wind and ev'ry kind of Weather imagineable will put a Quietus upon Ops and create great Whining in the Corps of Pilots. "Oh FFS the Cross-wind blew me plane right offada runway!" shall N00bs complain, thence to learn the use of counteracting Rudder and the need for further Computer Upgrades. So sayeth the Oracle and thou knowest it to be true.

Eight. Aircraft in Formation shall by their Absence be conspicuous across the Skye. Sad though this be, yet evenso speaketh the Oracle.

Nine. Newfangled Graphics Cards shall continue to be required of N00bs ever and anon, carving greate Holes in their Budget or Allowance, for the Holy Recommended System Spec shalt for ever more lure them on to further Purchase. So proclaimeth the Oracle, in league with Developers and Hardware Vendors.

Ten. N00bhood shall wax Eternal, for such is the way of Man. Transcedence from one Stage to another shalt remain paineful and arduous despite Literature and Training Programmes. Fearest thou not for that is good, as Pukes and Vets shall always require fresh Baby Seal Meat upon their platters. Thus spake the Oracle and bade his Adieu, "Fare Thee Well!"

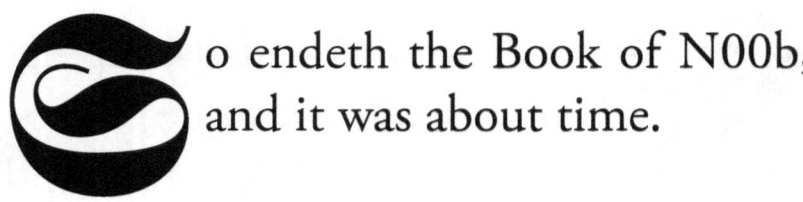

o endeth the Book of N00b, and it was about time.

ABOUT THE AUTHOR

Born 1963 in Sweden, Johan "BMBM" Kylander is a marketing executive with a second life in the realm of massively multiplayer online flight simulation. Gaining his wings in Air Warrior and WarBirds™, he eventually progressed to the all-arms simulation WWII Online: Battlefield Europe where he made a name for himself as a premier fighter pilot and formation leader. His online career stretched from 1996 to 2004 when he retired to pursue his Real Life™ and write about air combat. Johan "BMBM" Kylander is the author of "In Pursuit – A Pilot's Guide to Online Air Combat" which has received wide acclaim as the "must-have" book for aspiring flight-sim junkies.

www.ingramcontent.com/pod-product-compliance
Lightning Source LLC
Chambersburg PA
CBHW031853170626
46807CB00004B/1713